Kids *make* America *great again*

Frank Nato

To order additional copies of this book, contact:
Xlibris
844-714-8691
www.Xlibris.com
Orders@Xlibris.com

ISBN: Softcover   978-1-6641-8272-1
       Hardcover   978-1-6641-8273-8
       EBook   978-1-6641-8271-4

Print information available on the last page

Rev. date: 07/09/2021

Kids *make* America *great again*

During the seismic corona pandemic, a lot of parents were sad, depressed, petrified, and beleaguered because of work denied, job application rejected, and their financial situation going sour.

Oprah and Ariana wanted to rescue the situation.

Their teacher had explained everything. Their teacher had explained everything about why the planes halted. He had said that washing hands and standing six feet apart could rescue a life.

On a scale, sanitizing serious, idle hands meant stress more than greasy, sweaty, and busy hands.

Oprah and Ariana empathized and sympathized their parents. A lot of parents were jobless. The community was silently getting worried. The country needed leadership from the man elected as president.

Oprah and Ariana did not need anything from the top leadership. Leadership could come from the bottom up.

"I have an idea, Ariana."

"What is it that you are thinking?" Ariana wondered.

"We cannot stay here and watch our parents struggle financially."

"Certainly."

"We have to do something."

"What did you have in mind?"

"This is the plan."

And they agreed.

The following morning, they explained their idea to their parents. Their mom and dad agreed as long as they kept safe.

They fetched their tools, rolled up their sleeves, and started work immediately.

They worked for a cheaper labor and worked plenty of hours.

They were happy working, motivated and with passion.

Word of mouth spread around. Interested people visited their website, asking for cheaper service, and in return, they made a few dollars.

Early morning, the president got information about the kids from his handlers. He learned that they had made people smile with their cheap labor during the pandemic.

They were trending because they gave people a welcome respite through hard work.

The president was happy and asked his handlers to invite them at the White House. He wanted to thank them for their motivation and hard work.

Coincidentally, the White House lawn needed some mowing. The president asked if they could provide their services.

They borrowed patriotism akin to soldiers armed with arsenal and sophisticated weapon to serve. They borrowed patriotism akin to doctors armed with syringe and mask.

They agreed to mow the White House lawn armed with sixteenth-century invention, like the wheelbarrow, rake, leaf blower, and mowing machine.

After a whole day's work, the president did not mention about the payment method. He decided he wouldn't pay and couldn't pay. And he had other ways to honor them.

"You have done a fantastic job, girls. Your patriotism will be recognized when the history of this land is mentioned. You have done a fantastic job, and we feel privileged to associate with you. This had been a tremendous job, and you have given it your all to serve this nation. I would like to thank you again. If there is anything I could do for you, just mention it."

The girls were embarrassed to ask for payment because on a scale that they had to choose between money and patriotism, they chose silence.

The minister of finance had budgeted millions of shillings to go into mowing the White House lawn and other millions to solve and maintain plumbing, electricity, roofing, and other services so the White House could host dignitaries in the most tranquil environment.

But the money seemed to be in the wrong hands, perhaps stashed away in a safe.

The media enlightened the citizens. They reported about the mischief because it was the duty of the National Park Service to maintain the White House lawn.

They had sophisticated tools, like the Grasshopper mower. But the president opted for cheaper laborers.

Oprah and Ariana never got a dime after a whole day's work.

The media tried to ask them questions. Ariana and Oprah tried to keep away from politics. They never said any word but kept on looking for interested customers. They just wanted to mow lawn grass.

Angry citizens came out to protest. They wanted justice and the girls' pay.

The media reported that the leadership needed more mowing, oiling, and greasing because the wheels of the mower machine were moving faster than the wheels of integrity.

The president ignored their cry for sympathy. He tweeted about the next election. He wanted to win another second term to conclude what he had begun.

The citizens began a GoFundMe page for Oprah and Ariana.

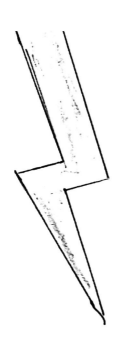

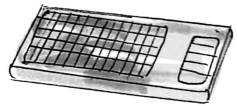

Then the people came out in huge numbers to vote, armed with vengeance, anger, and regret. They knew the person to vote for.

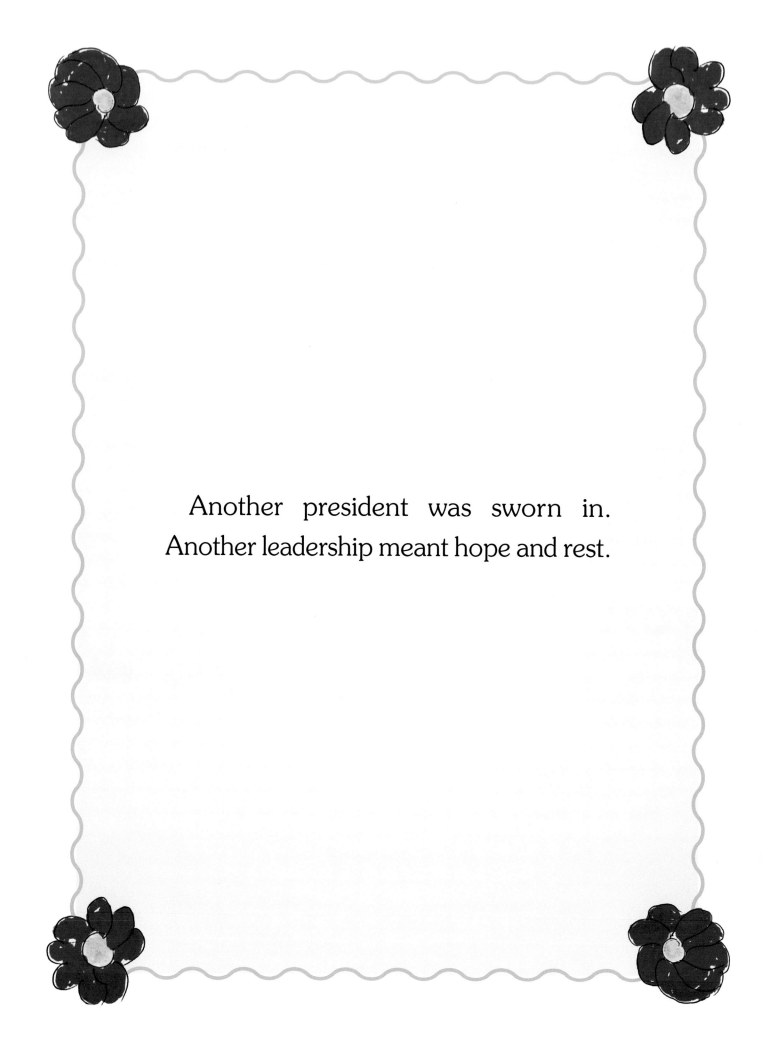

Another president was sworn in.
Another leadership meant hope and rest.

Oprah and Ariana went on a vacation.

"I guess we made America great again," Ariana joked.

"No, we made the yard great again," Oprah answered.

Printed in the United States
by Baker & Taylor Publisher Services